To:
From:

How to Catch a Yeti

From the
New York Times
Bestselling Team

Adam Wallace &
Andy Elkerton

sourcebooks
wonderland

Legend has it, there lives a beast
we really want to meet.
He's extra huge with snow-white fur,
and giant, fuzzy feet!

I know the Yeti does exist,
and I can prove it too!
So with my friends, we'll find him ***fast***
before the day is through!

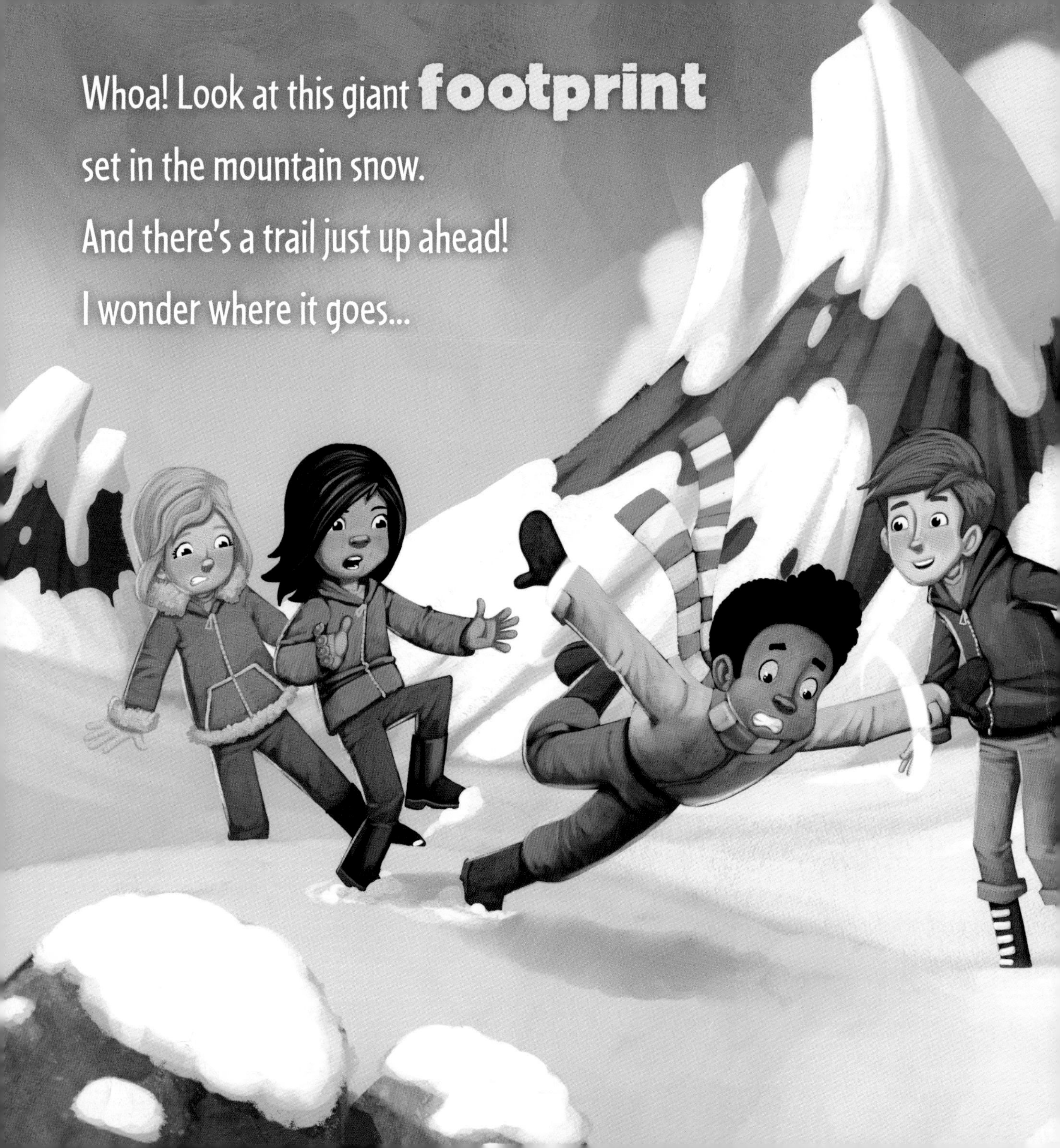

Whoa! Look at this giant **footprint**
set in the mountain snow.
And there's a trail just up ahead!
I wonder where it goes...

Is that a Yeti photograph?
How did that get there?
Hey! That's the beast we're looking for!
We must be in his LAiR!!!

I knew it, I knew it! He *does* exist!

Our **Yeti friend** is real!

And look, look, look! Just over there–

I swear I saw his heel!

Can we catch the Yeti?

You bet we're going to try!

Our **crystal snowflakes** might have worked,

but the Yeti said "bye bye!"

Syrup? Check. Candy? Check.

We'll catch the Yeti, no doubt!

Unless the Yeti's very **HUNGRY**...

Whoops! He just got out.

Quick! He went into that room!

We're gonna catch him now!

Eep! Where'd he go? That tricky dude!

He **ESCAPED** again—but how?

SWOOOOOOOOOOSh!

We thought that marbles, sleds, and snow
would finally do the trick.
But Yeti's moves are off the charts!
That dude is really SLICK!
dip
KA-POW!

This crystal cave is glowing bright!
I love the colored lights!
Too bad our bubbles didn't work.
We forgot about the stalactites!

POP!
POP!
POP!
POP!

Grab your gear—we've got this, guys!
Don't forget to aim!
We finally have a trap to win
this Yeti-catching **game!**

SPLAT!
SPLAT!
SPLAT!

I thought for sure that this would work,
But the **Yeti** got away.
I've got an idea that just can't lose.
One more shot, what do you say!?

Okay, this is our final chance! We haven't caught him...yet.

Our **Yeti Snatch-a-roo 3000™**

will catch him quick, no sweat!

Pop!
SPLAT!
Zzt!
Tzt!

Our Snatch-a-roo was just too slow,
and Yeti is too fast.
Even though we missed our friend,
today we've had a **BLAST!**

...zZZzzzzzzzzzzzzt...

YETI
"Thanks for playing, kids!" he says,
"Those traps were so much fun.
Please come back and play again,
our friendship's just begun!"

Come again soon!

Text by Adam Wallace
Illustrations by Andy Elkerton

The art was first sketched, then painted digitally with brushes designed by the artist.

Published by Sourcebooks Wonderland, an imprint of Sourcebooks Kids
P.O. Box 4410, Naperville, Illinois 60567-4410
(630) 961-3900
sourcebookskids.com

Library of Congress Cataloging-in-Publication Data is on file with the publisher.
Source of Production: Worzalla, Stevens Point, Wisconsin, USA
Date of Production: August 2020
Run Number: 5019503

Printed and bound in the United States of America.

WOZ 10 9 8 7 6 5 4 3